BARTERING

Nicolas Brasch

Australia • Brazil • Japan • Korea • Mexico • Singapore • Spain • United Kingdom • United States

Bartering

Fast Forward
Blue Level 11

Text: Nicolas Brasch
Illustrations: Vaughan Duck
Editor: Kate McGough
Design: Vonda Pestana
Series design: James Lowe
Production controller: Emma Hayes
Photo research: Gillian Cardinal
Reprint: Jennifer Foo
Audio recordings: Juliet Hill, Picture Start
Spoken by: Matthew King and Abbe Holmes

Acknowledgements
The author and publisher would like to acknowledge permission to reproduce material from the following sources:

Photographs by Alamy Images, pp 13, 15 top; photolibrary.com/Index Stock, p 12.

ISBN 978 0 17 012559 8
ISBN 978 0 17 012549 9 (set)

Cengage Learning Australia
Level 7, 80 Dorcas Street
South Melbourne, Victoria Australia 3205
Phone: 1300 790 853

Cengage Learning New Zealand
Unit 4B Rosedale Office Park
331 Rosedale Road, Albany, North Shore NZ 0632
Phone: 0800 449 725

For learning solutions, visit **cengage.com.au**

Printed in Australia by Ligare Pty Ltd
5 6 7 8 9 10 11 20 19 18 17 16

THE UNIVERSITY OF MELBOURNE

Evaluated in independent research by staff from the Department of Language, Literacy and Arts Education at the University of Melbourne.

BARTERING

Nicolas Brasch

Contents

Chapter 1

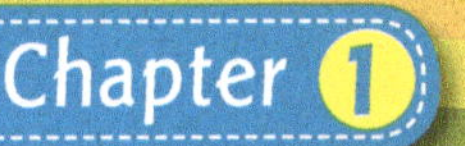

WHAT IS BARTERING?

Bartering is when people swap one kind of **good** or **service** for another.

Bartering needs two people to make it work. Each person needs to have something that the other person wants.

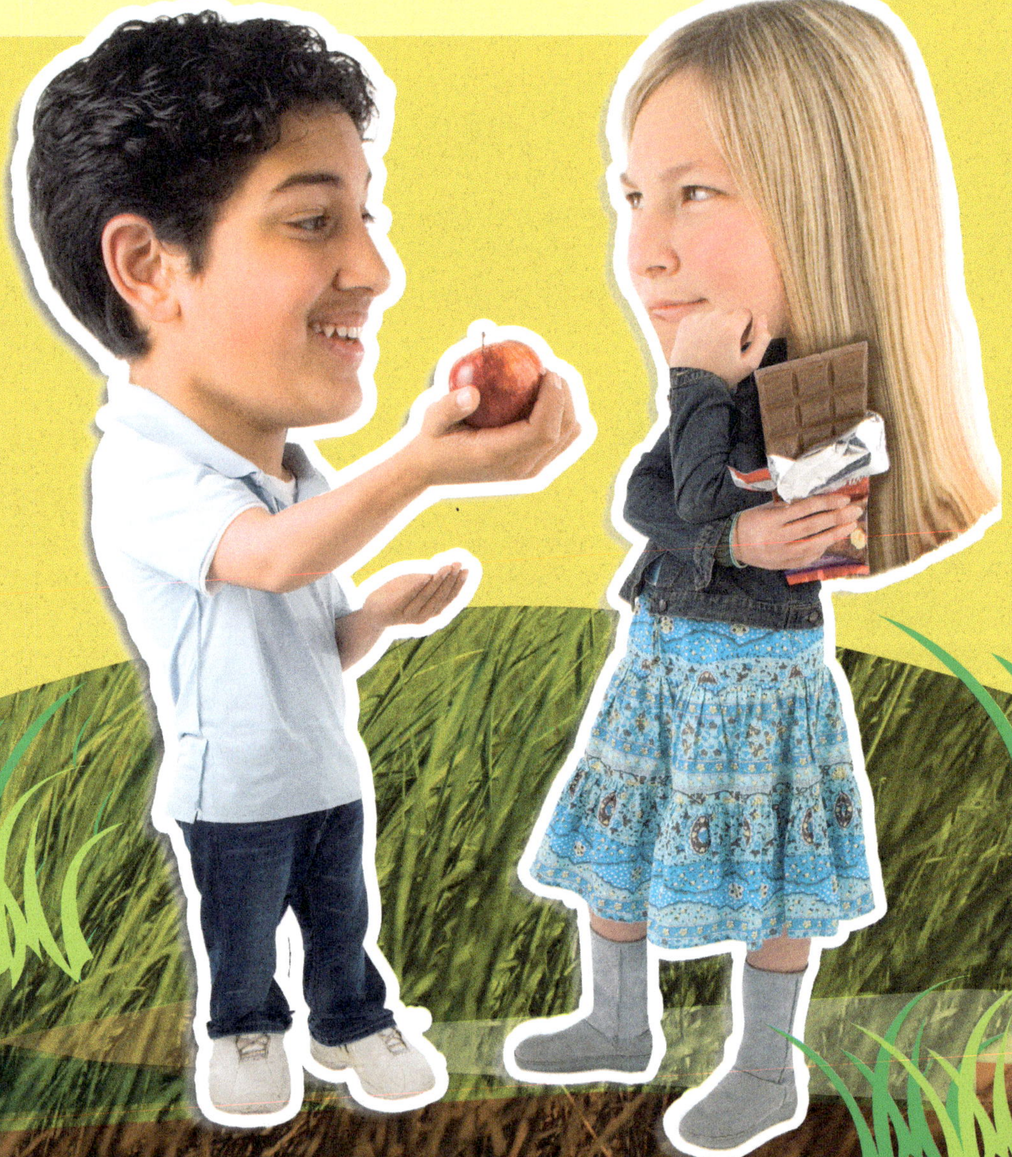

This boy has a swap card that the girl wants.
The girl has a swap card that the boy has wanted for a long time.
They swap cards.
This is bartering.

A LONG HISTORY

People have been buying goods and services with money for more than 2500 years.
But, people have been bartering for much longer.

When **communities** were small, bartering worked well. It was easy to swap one good for another or one service for another.

People didn't need money to buy what they needed.

But then communities grew bigger.
This made bartering harder
because there were more people.
So people started buying goods and services
with money.

Over the years, countries have also bartered with one another.

Sometimes, countries swap goods.

One country may have a lot of wool from their sheep.
The other country may make a lot of TVs.
So the countries swap wool for TVs.
TRALIA

Chapter 3

BARTERING TODAY

Today, most people buy goods and services with money. But bartering still goes on.

A person may swap an orange for an apple with a friend. This is bartering.

Someone may paint a person's room for a ride to work. This is bartering.

Someone may cut a friend's grass for fixing their car.
This is bartering.

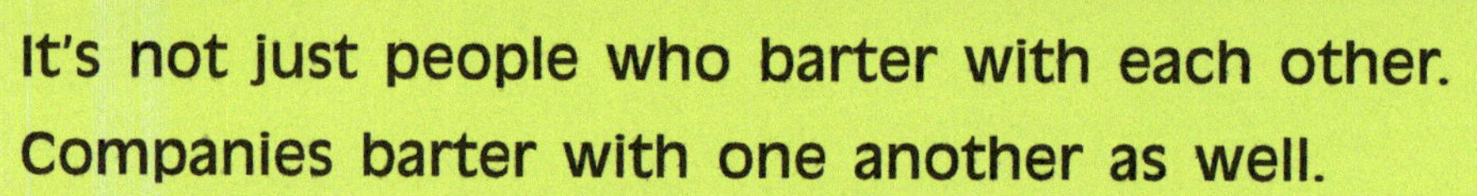
It's not just people who barter with each other.
Companies barter with one another as well.

A cleaning company may clean the rooms in a hotel.
The hotel may then let people from the cleaning company stay in the hotel for free.
Both the cleaning company and the hotel have got what they want without needing money.

This is bartering.

FAST FACTS

Bartering is when people swap one kind of good or service for another.

Bartering was around before money.

Bartering needs two people to make it work.

Each person needs to have something that the other person wants.

It's not only people who barter with one another.
Companies barter with one another as well.
Over the years, even countries have bartered with one another.

Glossary

communities groups of people living together in one place

good a thing or possession used to barter with

service something a person or company does for someone else

Index